James A. Wineberger

The Home of Washington at Mount Vernon

embracing a full and accurate description

James A. Wineberger

The Home of Washington at Mount Vernon
embracing a full and accurate description

ISBN/EAN: 9783337287672

Printed in Europe, USA, Canada, Australia, Japan

Cover: Foto ©Andreas Hilbeck / pixelio.de

More available books at **www.hansebooks.com**

THE

HOME OF WASHINGTON

AT

MOUNT VERNON,

EMBRACING A

FULL AND ACCURATE DESCRIPTION,

AS WELL AS OF

The Birthplace, Genealogy, Character, Marriage, and
Last Illness of Washington,

together with

INCIDENTS PERTAINING TO THE BURIAL OF WASHINGTON, REMO-
VAL FROM THE OLD FAMILY VAULT, AND HIS BEING PLACED
IN THE NEW TOMB, IN A MARBLE SARCOPHAGUS.

BY J. A. WINEBERGER.

WASHINGTON:
THOMAS McGILL, PRINTER.
1860.

The author is under obligations to JOHN A. WASHINGTON, Esq., of Mount Vernon; the late G. W. P. CUSTIS, Esq., of Arlington, Va.; and REMBRANDT PEALE, Esq., of Philadelphia, for many facts contained within these pages.

C. W. MURRAY, STEREOTYPER,
WASHINGTON, D. C.

TABLE OF CONTENTS.

I.

Mount Vernon.

"There rests the Man, the flower of human kind,
　Whose visage mild bespoke his nobler mind;
There rests the Soldier, who his sword ne'er drew
　But in a righteous cause, to Freedom true;
There rests the Hero, who ne'er fought for fame,
　Yet gained more glory than a Cæsar's name;
There rests the Statesman, who, devoid of art,
　Gave soundest counsels from an upright heart.
And, O Columbia! by thy sons caress'd,
　There rests the Father of the realms he bless'd,
Who no wish felt to make his mighty praise,
　Like other Chiefs, the means himself to raise;
But when retiring, breathed in pure renown,
　And felt a grandeur that disdained a crown."

MOUNT VERNON has a deep and enduring interest
for those who esteem the memory of Washington. It
is a Mecca, towards which the heart turns with intense
emotion, and which every American may visit to commemorate the virtues of his country's greatest benefactor, upon whose character and history he may meditate
until, from the suggestions of the past, as memory brings
them up, link by link, he may catch something of the
spirit of the mighty dead. Here the lessons of patriot-

ism may be enhanced, the mind elevated to nobler views
of the vital questions that concern our country's welfare, the elements of our pure institutions brought to
remembrance, and the tone of public life in former generations recalled.

Ten miles below Alexandria, and sixteen below
Washington City, the majestic waters of the Potomac
lave the shore of Mount Vernon.

The present owner of Mount Vernon is John A.
Washington, Esq., (the 3d,) the great-grand nephew of
General Washington. He inherited the estate from
his father, John A. Washington, (the 2d.) The latter
was the nephew of Judge Bushrod Washington, who
appointed him one of his executors, and bequeathed
him the estate, on which he died, June 16th, 1832,
aged 43.

Judge Bushrod Washington was the son of John A.
Washington, (the 1st,) and nephew of General Washington, who appointed him one of his executors, and
bequeathed him the estate. He died in Philadelphia,
November 26th, 1829, aged 68, having been for thirty
years an Associate Justice of the Supreme Court of the
United States, which situation he held at the time of
his death.

General Washington was appointed, in the will of

his half-brother, Lawrence, one of his executors, and the
estate, bequeathed to his surviving daughter, Sarah, was
to pass to the General if she died without issue; and he
therefore came in possession of the same July 26th,
1752. He made extensive improvements, and enlarged
the estate, of which he set apart a considerable quan-
tity for cultivation during his lifetime. At his death
—he dying without issue—he gave and bequeathed to
his wife the benefit of all his real and personal property
during her natural life, with the exception of some
special bequests which he made to some of his relatives and most intimate friends, not on account of their
intrinsic value, but as tokens of his high respect. Among
these were: A box made of the oak that sheltered
Sir William Wallace after the battle of Falkirk, originally designed to be presented by the Goldsmith's Com-
pany of Edinburgh to Lord Buchan, who received it
upon condition that it might be transferred to General
Washington, who recommitted it by bequest to Lord
Buchan, and in case of his death to his heir.

To his brother, Charles Washington, he gave his gold-
headed cane, left to him by Dr. Benjamin Franklin in
his will.

To Lawrence and Robert Washington, of Chotanck,
King George's county, Va., "acquaintances and

friends of his juvenile years," he gave his other two
gold-headed canes, with his arms engraved upon them,
one to each ; also two spy-glasses, one to each.   The
spy-glasses, he said, constituted part of his equipment
during the Revolutionary war.

To his compatriot in arms, his old intimate friend
and family physician, Dr. James Craik, he gave his
secretary and circular chair.   These were appendages
to his study room.

To Dr. David Stuart he gave his large shaving and
dressing table and his telescope.

To Lord Fairfax he gave a Bible in three large folio
volumes, presented to him by the Rev. Thomas Wilson,
Bishop of Sodor and Man, England.

To General De Lafayette he gave a pair of finely-
wrought steel pistols, which were taken from the British in the Revolutionary war.

To five of his nephews—William Augustine Washington, George Lewis, George Steptoe Washington,
Bushrod Washington, and Samuel Washington—he
bequeathed a sword to each, adding the injunction not
to take them from their scabbards with the intention
of shedding blood, except in self-defence or in defence
of their country, and, in the latter case, to keep them
unsheathed and die with them in their hands rather

than give up the same. Some of these swords were worn by his side in his engagements with the enemies of his country.

To his nephew, Busbrod Washington, he bequeathed all his civil and military papers. These were purchased by Congress, and are now in the archives of the departments. Also his private papers and the books of every description in his library.

To his wife and her heirs forever he bequeathed an improved town lot in Alexandria and his household furniture of every kind.

By his will his whole real estate, amounting nearly to ten thousand acres of land, was divided, after the death of his wife, among the following recipients:

First. To his nephew, Busbrod Washington, and his heirs, he gave and bequeathed Mount Vernon, (proper,) which contained upwards of four thousand acres of land, together with the mansion and all other buildings and improvements, as Washington said, " partly in consideration of an intimation to his deceased father, while we were bachelors, and he had kindly undertaken to superintend my estate during my military services in the former war between Great Britain and France, that, if I should fall therein. Mount Vernon, then less ex-

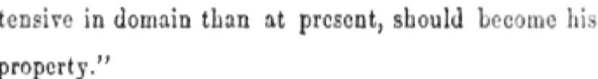

tensive in domain than at present, should become his property."

Second. To George Fayette Washington and Charles Augustine Washington he gave and bequeathed, to them and their heirs, the estate east of Little Hunting creek, bordering on the Potomac river, containing upwards of two thousand acres. In giving this bequest he said : "In consideration of the consanguinity between them and my wife, being as nearly related to her as to myself, as on account of the affection I had for and the obligation I was under to their father when living, who from his youth had attached himself to my person and followed my fortunes through the vicissitudes of the late Revolution, afterwards devoting his time to the superintendence of my private concerns for many years, whilst my public employments rendered it impracticable for me to do it myself, thereby affording me essential services, and always performing them in a manner the most filial and respectful."

Third. To his nephew, Lawrence Lewis, and Eleanor Parke Lewis, his wife, and their heirs, he gave and bequeathed the residue of the domain of the Mount Vernon estate not already devised to his nephew, Bushrod Washington, and a tract of land west of this, together with a mill, distillery, and other improvements on the premises, both together making about two thousand acres. In giving this he said : " And whereas it has always been my intention, since my expectation of having issue ceased, to consider the grandchildren of my wife in the same light as I do my own relations, and to act a friendly part by them ; more especially by the two whom we have raised from their earliest infancy, namely, Eleanor Parke Custis and George Washington Parke Custis; and whereas the former of these hath lately intermarried with Lawrence Lewis, a son of my deceased sister, Betty Lewis, by which union the inducement to provide for them both has been increased."

Fourth. To his ward, who was also his wife's grandson, George Washington Parke Custis, and his heirs, he bequeathed a tract of land on Four-Mile run, near Alexandria, containing one thousand two hundred acres, also his entire square No. 21 in the city of Washington. In giving this, he said he was actuated by the principle already mentioned—that is, considering the grandchildren of his wife in the same light as he did his own relations.

Fifth. The balance of his real and personal estate, accompanied by a schedule and a reasonable estimate of its value, he desired might be sold by his executors,* if they could not agree otherwise in the division.

Lastly. He generously gave freedom to all the slaves he owned, and made ample provision for the helpless ones, both old and young.

---

* The executors were his wife, Martha Washington, his nephews, William Augustine Washington, Bushrod Washington, George Steptoe Washington, Samuel Washington, and Lawrence Lewis, and his ward, George Washington Parke Custis.

II.

Patentees of Mount Vernon.

The Mount Vernon estate was originally the half of 5,000 acres of land that was assigned, on division, to John Washington, the great-grandfather of General Washington, who, in conjunction with Nicholas Spencer, patented it from Lord Culpeper in 1670. John Washington bequeathed this estate to his son Lawrence, who bequeathed it to his son Augustine, who bequeathed it to his son Lawrence, who gave it the name it now bears, in honor of High Admiral Vernon, of the British navy, under whom Lawrence had served. Lawrence bequeathed it to his half-brother, George, as has already been stated.

III.

Origin and Genealogy.

The family name of Washington is derived from a person originally named William De Hertburn, whose name was changed in the 13th century, from the fact of his owning a manor called Washington, in the county of Durham, in England, where a custom prevailed in those days to name the person after his estate.

The name became conspicuous in the local history of England, which has uniformly spoken of the family as being composed of individuals of the highest respectability, possessing wealth, talent, and influence.

Sir Henry Washington, one of the family, a British colonel, made himself renowned for the active part he sustained at the capture of Bristol, in 1640, in the army of Charles I. Two uncles of this Colonel Washington came together to this country—John, the original owner of the land now called Mount Vernon, and his brother Lawrence—from England, in the year 1657, and settled upon the banks of Bridge's (afterwards called Pope's) creek, in the colony of Virginia.

IV.

Marriages and Deaths.

John Washington, soon after he came to America, was appointed to a military command against the Indians, and was afterwards raised to the rank of a colonel. He married Anne Pope, by whom he had two sons, Lawrence and John, and a daughter, named Anne, who married Major Francis Wright.

Lawrence, the eldest son of John and Anne, married Mildred Warner, daughter of Col. Augustine Warner, of Westmoreland county, Virginia, and had two sons, John and Augustine, and a daughter, named Mildred, who married for her first husband a Mr. Gregory, and for her second Col. Henry Willis, by the latter of whom only she had issue.

John, the eldest son of Lawrence and Mildred, married Catharine Whiting, of Gloucester county, in which he settled, died, and was buried. He left two sons, Warner and Henry, and three daughters, Mildred, Elizabeth, and Catharine.

THE FATHER OF WASHINGTON,

Augustine, the youngest son of Lawrence and Mildred, married, on the 20th April, 1715, Jane Butler,

the daughter of Col. Caleb Butler, of Westmoreland
county, Va. She died November 24th, 1728, and was
buried in the family vault at Bridge's creek. She left
three sons, Butler, Lawrence, and Augustine, and a
daughter, Jane; Butler and Jane died quite young.
Their father married, March 6th, 1730, for his second
wife, Mary Ball, by whom he had six children,
George, the illustrious patriot, Betty, Samuel, John
Augustine, Charles, and Mildred. The latter died
when an infant. Augustine (the hero's sire) died
April 12, 1743. Sparks says:

"Little is known of his acts. It appears by his
will, however, that he possessed a large and valuable
property in lands; and as this had been acquired chiefly
by his own enterprise, it may be inferred that in the
concerns of business he was methodical, skilful, honor-
able, and energetic. His occupation was that of a
planter, which, from the first settlement of the country,
had been the pursuit of nearly all the principal gentlemen of Virginia. Each of his sons inherited from him
a separate plantation. It is thus seen that Augustine
Washington, although suddenly cut off in the vigor of
manhood, left all his children in a state of comparative
independence. Confiding in the prudence of the mother,
he directed that all the proceeds of the property of her

children should be at her disposal till they should respectively come of age."

To his son Lawrence he gave the Mount Vernon estate, together with lands and shares in iron works which were very valuable in Virginia and Maryland.

To Augustine he gave the old home farm at Bridge's creek, the place where he was buried, in the tomb of his ancestors.

To George he gave the new home farm, opposite Fredericksburg, on the east side of the Rappahannock river, the place where he lived at the time of his death.

To the rest of his sons he gave each a separate estate of from six to seven hundred acres.

For his only remaining daughter, Betty, ample provision was made in his will.

THE MOTHER OF WASHINGTON,

Mary, the widow of Augustine, General Washington's mother, died in Fredericksburg, August 25th, 1789, at the age of 82. She was buried upon the estate (adjoining Fredericksburg) of her son-in-law, Col. Fielding Lewis, on an elevated spot, which was selected by her for the purpose a number of years previous to her death.

"Within a few steps from the place where she lies interred is a romantic ledge of rocks to which she used often to resort for private meditation and devotion. She was a lady of uncommon excellence, and was greatly endeared to all who had the happiness of her acquaintance. She was truly estimable in all the relations of life; but among the distinguished traits of her character, none was more remarkable than her constant and generous attentions to the necessities of the poor. She for years was expecting the approach of death from a deep-rooted cancer in her breast, and was long desirous to lay aside her clayey tabernacle to depart and be with Christ, in whom was all her hope; yet she was enabled to exercise a becoming resignation to the will of God under all the sufferings she endured from her excruciating disorder." Over her grave is now to be seen a half-finished white marble monument, (presenting rather an imposing aspect, notwithstanding its unfinished state,) the corner-stone of which was laid May 7th, 1833, by General Andrew Jackson, then President of the United States.

LAWRENCE WASHINGTON.

Lawrence, the eldest son then living of Augustine and Jane, married, July 19th, 1743, Anne, eldest daughter of the Hon. William Fairfax, who was a distant relative of Lord Fairfax. They had four children ; three died young, and the other lived some time after the death of her father : he died in 1752, aged 34, and was placed in the family vault at Mount Vernon.

V.

Washington's Marriage.

George, the eldest son of Augustine and Mary, married, January 6th, 1758, Martha Custis, widow of Daniel Parke Custis, and daughter of John Dandridge, of New Kent county, Virginia.* The marriage took place on the banks of the Pomunkey, a branch of the York river, in New Kent county. The ceremony was performed by the Rev. Mr. Munson, who was the rector of St. Peter's church. "This union," says Sparks, "was in every respect felicitous. It continued forty years. To her intimate acquaintances and to the nation the character of Mrs. Washington was ever a theme of praise. Affable and courteous, exemplary in her deportment, remarkable for her deeds of charity and

---

* Mrs. Custis had two children living at the time of her second marriage—one a son (named John) 6 years old; the other a daughter (named Martha) two years younger. The son afterwards became aid-de-camp to General Washington, and during the seige of Yorktown was seized with a camp fever, then raging in the British entrenchments, from the effects of which he died, in the 27th year of his age, at his home, Eltham, in New Kent county, whither he had been removed. He was the father of the late and highly esteemed G. W. P. Custis, of Arlington, Va. The daughter died in her 19th year at Mount Vernon.

piety, unostentatious, and without vanity, she adorned by her domestic virtues the sphere of private life, and filled with dignity every station in which she was placed." She was noted for her beauty and accomplishments, and possessed considerable wealth.

Soon after their marriage they moved to Mount Vernon, and there permanently settled.

VI.

Washington's Courtship.

It was in the month of May, 1758, when Washington, (then a Colonel,) being on his way to Williamsburg
from Winchester, then his headquarters, on official business, was accosted by Mr. Chamberlyne—living in the
mansion known as the White House, situated on the
southern side of the Pomunkey river, near Williams'
Ferry, in Kent county—who insisted upon his stopping
and partaking of his hospitality during the day. The
Colonel apologized by saying his time would not permit;
but, Mr Chamberlyne offering, as an inducement, the
promise of an introduction to *"a young widow"* who
was then under his roof, he waived his objections and
consented to stay until after dinner. Orders were given
accordingly to the Colonel's attendant—a body servant,
bequeathed, with a noble charger, to Washington,
by General Braddock in his dying moments. On being ushered into the house, he was introduced to several
guests, and among the rest the fascinating young widow.
The result of their interview was a mutual reciproca-
tion of the tender feeling. He dined, and the servant
was ready with the charger; but love induced procras-

tination. Time passed on, and yet the Colonel did not appear; the servant meanwhile wondering at his unusual delay, as he was noted for his great punctuality. The host at length ordered the horses to be put up for the night, as no guest left his house after sundown. The next morning late, the Colonel put spurs to his charger, and, having reached the seat of government, soon dispatched his business, and returned again to Mr. Chamberlyne's mansion, where an engagement was entered into and preparations made for the marriage. Mr. G. W. P. Custis said he had often "heard of that marriage, from the gray-haired domestics who waited at the board where love made the feast and Washington the guest. And rare and high was the revelry at that palmy period of Virginia's festal age; for many were gathered to that marriage, of the good, the great; and they, with joyous acclamations, hailed in Virginia's youthful hero a happy and prosperous bridegroom."

" 'And so you remember when Colonel Washington came a courting of your young mistress?' said Mr. Custis to old Cully, in his hundredth year. 'Ay, master, that I do,' replied the ancient family servant, who had lived to see five generations; 'great times, sir, great times—shall never see the like again.' 'And Washington looked something like a man, a proper man

—hey, Cully?' 'Never seed the like, sir—never the like of him, though I have seen many in my day—so tall, so straight! and then he sat on a horse and rode with such an air! Ah, sir, he was like no one else. Many of the grandest gentlemen, in gold lace, were at the wedding; but none looked like the man himself.' Strong indeed must have been the impression which the person and manner of Washington made upon the 'rude, untutored mind' of this poor negro, since the lapse of three-quarters of a century had not sufficed to efface it."

VII.

The Birthplace of Washington.

Blest be the spot that gave thee birth,
　　Immortal Washington;
Thy name will ever shine on earth
　　Bright as the midday sun.

The birthplace of General Washington is in the parish of Washington—named after his great-grandfather, John—situated on a tolerably elevated plain, which commands a bold and majestic prospect of the Maryland shore and of the broad Potomac, extending many miles towards the Chesapeake bay. It is half a mile from the mouth and about sixty yards from the shore of Pope's creek, which flows gracefully on its course, around precipitous and crescent-formed banks, into the Potomac river, ninety miles south of Washington city, in the county of Westmoreland, Va. The spot is designated by a granite slab, now broken in three pieces, bearing this plain inscription, " Here, on the 11th of February,* 1732, George Washington was

---

* Old style, which corresponds to the 22d of February new style, the day celebrated as the anniversary of Washington's birth.

Washington was baptized on the 16th of April, 1732, accord-

born." The slab was placed there by George W. P. Custis, esq., in June, 1815.

Col. John Washington, who came from England and settled on Pope's creek, granted a tract of land at its mouth to his son Lawrence.

Lawrence, in his will, dated March 11th, 1698, says, "I give the tract of land on which I now live to my son, John Washington." There were also bequests made by him to his son Augustine and to his daughter Mildred. It appears from authentic information that John Washington sold this estate to his brother Augustine, the father of George, who bequeathed it to his son Augustine, who bequeathed it to his son William Augustine, who bequeathed it to his son, Col. George C. Washington, who sold it to John Gray, with the exception of a reservation of sixty feet square around the site of the house, which is memorable as being the birthplace of General Washington ; and a reservation of twenty feet square around the burial-ground and vault of the Washington family, situated about a mile from the site of the house, in which are interred the remains of the father, grandfather, and great-grand-

ing to the rites and ceremonies of the Protestant Episcopal church, which was the established church and the prevailing religion at that period in Virginia.

father of General Washington, and members of their respective families. A few partially decayed posts only remain of the old enclosure around this consecrated locality.

Near the vault is a moss-covered tombstone, having upon it the following inscription : "Here lyeth ye body of John Washington, eldest son to Captain Lawrence Washington, who departed this life ye 10th of January, 1690, aged 10 years and 6 mouths. Also Mildred Warner, eldest daughter to said Washington, who died ye 1st of August, 1696."

Lewis W. Washington, son and heir-at-law of Col. George C. Washington, presented these reservations "to the mother State of Virginia, in perpetuity, on condition solely that the State require the said places to be permanently enclosed with an iron fence based on stone foundations, together with suitable and modest (though substantial) tablets, to commemorate to the rising generation these notable spots."

The grant has been accepted by the State of Virginia, and the sum of $5,000 appropriated for the purpose of fulfilling the conditions mentioned, and erecting upon the sixty-foot lot consecrated as Washington's birthplace a memorial to the *Pater Patriæ*.

On the occasion of Gov. H. A. Wise's visit, April

27, 1858, in order to have the grounds surveyed as
granted to the State of Virginia, an aged person present remarked, " that he distinctly remembered when a
house occupied the spot where the chimney now stands,
and that it was used for a kitchen and laundry." Near
this place is plainly visible a filled-up cellar, having
chimney marks at each end, about sixty feet apart.
This is supposed to be the identical locality where the
house stood in which General Washington was born.
It was either burnt or pulled down previous to the
Revolutionary war.

Another aged gentleman living in the neighborhood
remembered the kind of house, and stated, years ago,
to Mr. J. K. Paulding, that the " house was a low-
pitched, single-storied, frame building, with four rooms
on the first floor, and an enormous chimney at each
end on the outside. 'This was the style of the better
sort of houses in those days, and they are still occasion-
ally seen in the old settlements of Virginia." '

Immediately beyond the chimney, and close by the
slab, a cluster of luxuriant fig trees have sprung up,
the parents of which yet exist in a decayed condition,
as remaining relics to point the traveler to the spot that
gave birth to Washington, which no American can ever
behold without feelings of the profoundest homage.

HOME MANSION.

VIII.

Mount Vernon Estate.

"On yonder swelling height,
    With ivied oaks and cedars crowned,
Where Freedom's banner floats in light,
    And every whispering sound
    Breathes of the past, 'tis consecrated ground.

"Pilgrim, ascend the steep,
    And there, with true and feeling heart,
On Vernon's brow deep silence keep;
    Ay, let the tear-drop start,
    While proud yet hallowed thoughts a balm impart!"

The Mount Vernon estate is located in the county of Fairfax, Va., on the western bank of the Potomac, commanding, from its situation, a magnificent and extended view of the meanderings of this lovely river in either direction for many miles.

It was bounded, when bequeathed to Judge Bushrod Washington, by the Potomac river; thence by Little Hunting creek as far up as Gum Spring on said creek; thence to a ford on Dogue run; thence along Dogue creek to the Potomac river.

THE MANSION HOUSE.

The mansion house,* consecrated as the home of

---

* Lawrence Washington built the central portion of the house, and the wings were added by General Washington

Washington, was built in accordance with the architec-
tural style then peculiar to the country, and is well
marked for its great simplicity and the excellence of
its general arrangements.   It stands upon an elliptical
plain, and has an elevation of at least two hundred feet
above the surface of the river, which is at this point
about two miles broad.   The mansion presents a fine
appearance in any position in which it may be viewed.
Built of the most durable frame-work, with all its fronts
cut in imitation of free-stone, its gray and time-worn
aspect is in contrast with houses of the present day,
with their newly-painted walls, green blinds, and nicely-
colored doors.   This edifice has withstood the ravages
of time remarkably well, as may be readily seen upon
inspection.   The house is two stories high, and is over-
topped with a slanting roof looking east and west, having three dormars eastward and two westward.   On
the first and second stories in the east façade or river
front are fourteen windows.   Upon the roof, in the
centre, is an octagonal cupola, answering the purposes
of an observatory.   There are on the ground floor six
rooms, the most of them wainscoted, and having large
worked cornices and shafts, in keeping with the taste
of former days.   The central building has a very roomy
hall on the same level with the pavement of the portico.

No doubt this hall was built by its original proprietor
that there might be ample room to receive guests in
that generous manner which prevailed among our Virginia ancestors. It has communication with three par-
lors and the main stairway, which leads to the chambers
in the second story, and above these to the observatory.

Attached to the house is a spacious portico fifteen
feet in width, its height reaching to the eaves of the
roof, having square pilasters. It extends entirely
across the eastern or river front, is ninety-six feet in
length, and has a light and graceful balustrade on its
top; its ground floor is paved with flat stone. Here
the hero used to walk, and here, doubtless, as his eye
glanced over the beautiful river, spreading out like a
bay at the foot of the hill, his mind was often filled
with reflections upon the alternate gloom and grandeur
of his country's early history, and with glowing con-
ceptions of the glorious future which awaited her.

The south wing of the building contains the library
and breakfast room, and a stairway that leads to Washington's private chamber on the second floor. The
library remains very much as when occupied by the
old hero. This wing has attached a porch facing the
south, giving an entrance to the house through the
library.

On the north wing is an extensive drawing-room,
decorated with a handsome mantel, presented in the
year 1785 to General Washington by Samuel Vaughen,
esq., of London, the father of the late and venerable
John Vaughen, of Philadelphia. The pillars are of a
rich variegated marble, partially set into the wall; the
other portion is composed of a fine white Italian marble,
having upon its freize, sculptured with a masterly hand
in bas-relief, prominent objects of agriculture and hus-
bandry, presenting a beautiful, gay, and graceful appearance.

The original mansion house, built by Lawrence Washington, forming the centre of the present building, con-
sisted only of four rooms upon each floor, to which its
present extent, with the numerous outbuildings attached, exhibits quite a contrast.

The improvements, such as the additions to the
house, the buildings around, and the laying off of the
gardens and grounds surrounding the premises, began
soon after peace was declared, in 1783, on Washington's return home from the seat of war.

There are many things of note and many highly-
esteemed relics in the house. Among these is an
ancient map of Virginia, representing the territory between the Atlantic ocean and the Ohio river, with pen-

cilled traces and marks from Washington's own hand, designating the route he traversed during Braddock's memorable and disastrous campaign against the French and Indians. The key of the Bastile is here, enclosed in a glass case placed on the wall in the hall. This key was sent by Lafayette from France to General Washington soon after the destruction of the prison. Upon a bracket over the door of the entrance into the library is a model bust, originally taken from life in a mask in plaster by M. Houdon, a French sculptor, who visited Mount Vernon in October, 1785, and spent three weeks there for the express purpose of procuring a likeness as exact in all its lineaments as his art and ingenuity could produce. The result is a work of art possessing much interest, as conveying a truly characteristic delineation and strongly-marked representation of the original, admitted without doubt to be the best likeness extant. This work was designed as a model from which to execute a statue of Washington for the State of Virginia, which authorized Franklin and Jefferson, then in Paris, to select an artist for this purpose. They chose M. Houdon. The statue is in the State Capitol at Richmond, Va.

The costume of this statue is the military dress of the Revolution. One hand holds a cane, the other rests upon the fasces, with which are united the sword and ploughshare, and over it a martial coat. The inscription, by James Madison, on the pedestal, is as follows:

"GEORGE WASHINGTON. The General Assembly of the Commonwealth of Virginia have caused this statue to be erected as a monument of affection and gratitude to GEORGE WASHINGTON; who, uniting to the endowments of the *hero* the virtues of the *patriot*, and exerting both in establishing the liberties of his country, has rendered his name dear to his fellow-citizens, and given the world an immortal example of true glory. Done in the year of Christ, one thousand seven hundred and eighty-eight, and in the year of the commonwealth the twelfth."

The following composition on the character of Washington, designed, perhaps, for a monumental inscription, was written, after Washington's death, on the back of a picture frame, in which is placed a miniature likeness of Washington, now hanging in the drawing room. The author gave in his name to the family as John Smith, of New York, but is supposed to have been an English traveller.

WASHINGTON,

The Defender of his Country—The Founder of Liberty—
The Friend of Man.
History and Tradition are explored in vain
For a Parallel to his Character.
In the Annals of Modern Greatness
He stands alone;
And the noblest names of antiquity lose their Lustre
In his Presence.

Born the Benefactor of Mankind,
He united all the qualities necessary to an illustrious career.
Nature made him great—He made himself virtuous.
Called by his country to the defence of her Liberties,
He triumphantly vindicated the rights of humanity,
And on the Pillars of National Independence
Laid the foundations of a great republic.

Twice invested with supreme magistracy
By the unanimous voice of a free people.
He surpassed in the Cabinet
The Glories of the Field,
And, voluntarily resigning the Sceptre and the Sword,
Retired to the shades of Private Life.

A spectacle so new and so sublime
Was contemplated with the profoundest admiration.
And the name of WASHINGTON,
Adding new lustre to humanity,
Resounded to the remotest regions of the earth.

Magnanimous in youth,
Glorious through life,
Great in Death,
His highest ambition the Happiness of Mankind,
His noblest Victory the conquest of himself,
Bequeathing to posterity the inheritance of his fame,
And building his monument in the hearts of his countrymen,
He Lived—The Ornament of the 18th Century;
He Died—Regretted by a Mourning World.

"All the regard one could wish seems to have been shown to the sacredness of these public relics, and all things have been kept very nearly as Washington left them.

"Money made in the stocks can purchase the bedizenry of our city drawing-rooms; but these elevating associations, which no gold can buy, no popular favor

win—which can only be inherited,—these are the heir-
looms, the traditionary titles and pensions, inalienable,
not conferred, which a republic allows to the descendants of her servants."

In visiting the mansion, and beholding the various
articles it contains, which were constantly in contact
with the great man, little effort is required to lead one
back to the days when there were assembled within its
walls those associates of his who laid the foundation of
our glorious Union.

Mr. Elkanah Watson, who visited Mount Vernon in
1785, arriving there in the afternoon of January 23d,
remarks that he observed a peculiarity in Washington's
smile, which seemed to illumine his eye; his whole
countenance beamed with intelligence, while it commanded confidence and respect.

The house on the west front has a very extensive
lawn, surrounded by serpentine walks, their borders
skirted in symmetry and beauty with the choicest forest trees, which were transplanted from the woods on the
estate, with evergreens and flowering shrubs, all selected,
planted, and attended by Washington. South of the
lawn, and a considerable distance from the left wing of
the house, is the vegetable garden; and opposite to
this, on the north of the lawn, about the same distance

from the right wing, are gardens and a conservatory for ornamental shrubs, plants, and flowers. These contain many valuable plants presented to Washington and preserved by him while living. Beyond the gardens and lawn is the orchard. The orchard, gardens, and conservatory were furnished with all varieties of rare fruits, vegetables, shrubs, and flowering plants, native and exotic. Horticulture was one of Washington's favorite pursuits, which he prosecuted with characteristic method and skill. Also on this front of the house are located negro quarters, seed houses, tool houses, and other buildings, the necessary appendages to a plantation. These things have no peculiar interest in themselves, except as belonging to the place, and being objects that received the owner's frequent attention.

IX

Summer House.

"How oft with placid eye
  Has he, whose spirit awes us still,
Stood where we stand, and viewed the sky,
  The river, vale, and hill,
  And heard the forest bird its anthem trill."

Upon the brow of the hill on which the mansion is situated, and not far from the water's edge, stands a frame, unfinished, square summer-house, and underneath an ice-house, both partially in ruins, in the rear of which is a beautiful lawn several acres in extent, reaching northward beyond the mansion, and planted with shrubbery and ornamental trees. A spectator has a fine view of the Potomac and Maryland shore from the summer house, which is the most conspicuous object seen in passing up the river, and presents a handsome appearance.

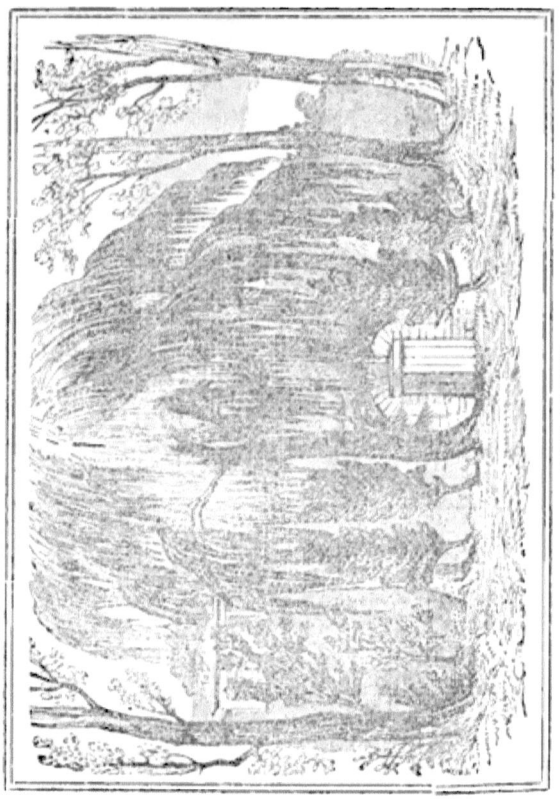

OLD TOMB.

X.

The Old Family Vault.

About two hundred and fifty yards south of the mansion house can be seen the old family vault, in a very dilapidated condition, situated on the ridge of a steep hill, embosomed among trees. It is arched with freestone, and over this a deep sod. Washington had contemplated moving this old family vault some time prior to his death, and in making his will he left a clause as follows : "The family vault at Mount Vernon requiring repairs, and being improperly situated besides, I desire that a new one, of brick, and upon a larger scale, may be built at the foot of what is commonly called the Vineyard Enclosure, on the ground, which is made out, in which my remains and those of my deceased relatives, (now in the old vault,) and such other of my family as may choose to be entombed there, may be deposited." But it was not finally done until an attempt was made some years ago to desecrate this hallowed spot by some demon in human form. The vault was entered, and a skull and other bones were taken from it. The robbery was discovered and the bones returned. The bones stolen, however, were not

those of the illustrious Washington.   The desire of
Washington in reference to the removal of the family
remains to the spot designated by him previous to his
death, and mentioned in his will, was carried out
through the agency of his nephew and friend, Major
Lewis, in 1831, or immediately after the robbery was
committed.   In the old vault the body of the Hero re-
mained from 1799 until 1831—a period over thirty-one
years.

NEW TOMB.

XI.

The New Vault.

"Nature hath marked the spot
    Where sleeps the great, the good, the wise,
Entombed—yet ne'er to be forgot :
    Ah, there the Hero lies !
    The man of mighty deeds and high emprise."

The new tomb is perhaps one hundred yards west of
the old vault, and three hundred southwest from the
mansion, on the hillside of a lovely retreat, and, though
not seen from the river, is suddenly brought into full
view as one ascends the long sloping hill from the
landing. This hallowed spot is surrounded by a deep
wooded dell containing thick shrubbery and many venerable, stately oaks, spreading their green foliage down
to the river banks.

The remains of the patriot and those of his wife lie
in marble sarcophagi, the two occupying (one on the
right side and the other on the left) a kind of antechamber, forming the entrance to the new vault, which
is visible from the outer gateway. This antechamber
is covered with a metallic roof, and its walls, built of
brick and elevated to the height of twelve feet, are so
extended in the rear as to surround the new vault on
all sides. Its front, which is surmounted with a stone

coping, is pierced by a gateway with a pointed gothic arch. The gate is composed of iron bars. Over the gateway is a plain slab, upon which are inscribed the words :

"WITHIN THIS ENCLOSURE REST THE REMAINS OF GENERAL GEORGE WASHINGTON."

The vault beyond the antechamber, where the body of the chief lay previously to the erection of the latter, (which was completed in 1837,) was built in 1831. The vault is arched over at the height of eight feet from the ground. Around this vault grew a few cedars, giving very little shade, many of the branches of which were lopped off by visitors as mementoes. The vault has a rough-cast front, with a plain iron door fixed in a free-stone casement. Over this there is a stone tablet, with the following brief passage from the Scriptures :

"I AM THE RESURRECTION AND THE LIFE ; HE THAT BELIEVETH IN ME, THOUGH HE WERE DEAD, YET SHALL HE LIVE."

The vault was constructed as it is seen at present, with the exception that the simple words " *Washington Family*" originally appeared upon a cap-stone, which the building of the antechamber made it necessary to remove.

In the lapse of more than thirty-one years the wooden

coffins have been three times renewed, and ultimately his friends succeeded in placing his ashes in a more durable receptacle.

Mr. John Struthers, a marble and granite cutter of Philadelphia, was consulted by the friends of Washington in reference to the construction of a marble sarcophagus to enshrine the remains of the illustrious chief. Mr. Struthers, with a deep feeling of respect and liberality, desired the privilege of constructing and presenting to the friends a sarcophagus made of Pennsylvania marble. It was granted; and in the execution of the work he has evidently displayed an unusual amount of artistic taste and skill. The following is a description of it :

"The construction of the sarcophagus is of the modern form, and consists of an excavation from a solid block of marble, eight feet in length, three feet in width, and two feet in height, resting on a plinth, which projects four inches round the base of the coffin. The lid or covering stone is a ponderous block of Italian marble, emblazoned with the arms and insignia of the United States, beautifully sculptured in the boldest relief. The design occupies a large portion of the central part of the top surface or lid, and represents a shield divided into thirteen perpendicular stripes, which

rests on the flag of our country, and is attached by
cords to a spear, embellished with tassels, forming a
background to the shield, by which it is supported.
The crest is an eagle with open wings, perching upon
the superior bar of the shield, and in the act of clutch-
ing the arrows and olive branch. Between these ar-
morial bearings and the foot of the coffin, upon the
plain field of the lid, is the bold and deeply-sculptured
name of

WASHINGTON."

At the foot of the coffin an inscription reads as follows :

BY THE PERMISSION OF LAWRENCE LEWIS, THE SURVIVING EXECUTOR OF
GEORGE WASHINGTON, THIS SARCOPHAGUS WAS PRESENTED BY
JOHN STRUTHERS, OF PHILADELPHIA, MARBLE MASON,
A. D. 1837.

The sarcophagus was intended to be placed in the
new vault, built in 1831; but Mr. Strickland, who
accompanied Mr. Struthers to Mount Vernon, says :

"Upon a consultation with this gentleman, [Major
Lewis,] after stating to him the difficulties which would
attend the placing of the sarcophagus in the damp
vault, and the inappropriateness of the situation for
such a work of art, and upon suggesting to him a plan
for constructing a suitable foundation on the right of
the entrance gate, on the outside of the vault, between

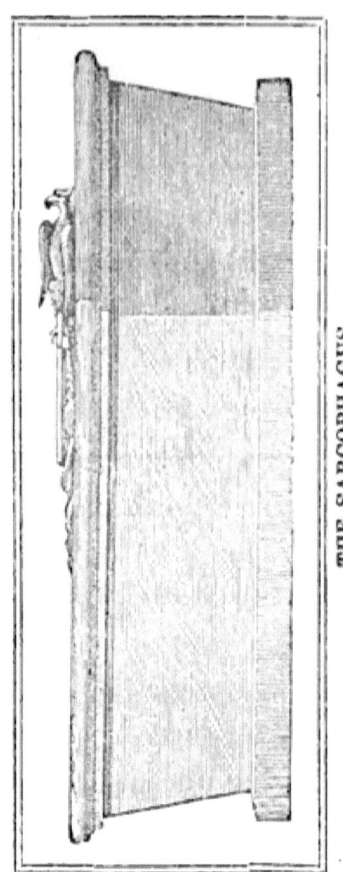

THE SARCOPHAGUS.

it and the surrounding walls, and the practicability of extending the side walls of the vault to the surrounding enclosure, and arching it over beyond any contact with the soil of the sloping hill, taking care to guard the vaulted chamber with a metallic roof, with an additional grille of iron bars in front, and other fastenings and securities, as guards against idle curiosity and the chances of attempt at desecration, he consented to the plan.

"We were accompanied to the spot by the steward, and the grated doors were opened for the first time in the lapse of seven years. During the operation the steward was directed to procure lights for the purpose of entering the vault and preparing the way for the removal of the body to the outside of the vault. The gate of the enclosure was temporarily closed, and upon the opening of the vault door we entered, accompanied by Major Lewis and his son. The coffin containing the remains of Washington was in the extreme back part of the vault; and to remove the case containing the leaden receptacle, it was found necessary to put aside the coffins that were piled up between it and the doorway. After clearing a passage-way, the case, which was much decayed, was stripped off, and the lead of the lid was discovered to have sunk very considerably from head to foot; so much so as to form a curved line of four to five inches in its whole length. This settlement of the metal had perhaps caused the soldering of the joints to give way about the upper or widest part of the coffin. The lead of the lid was restored to its place, and the body, raised by six men, was carried and laid in the marble coffin, and the ponderous cover being put on and set in cement, it was sealed from our sight on Saturday, the 7th day of October, 1837.

"Immediately after the performance of this melancholy ceremony, the sarcophagus was cased up with plank, to prevent any injury being done to the carving during the operation of enlarging the vault.

"The relatives, consisting of Major Lewis, Lorenzo Lewis, John Augustine Washington, Richard Blackburn Washington, George Washington, the Reverend Mr. Johnson and lady, and Miss Jane Washington, then retired to the mansion.

"The deepest feeling of reverence pervaded this assembly. The descendants of this illustrious man had the inexpressible satisfaction of seeing his ashes imperishably secured from the slow but sure attack of time.

"It is proper here to remark, that when the wooden case was removed from the leaden coffin, a silver breast-

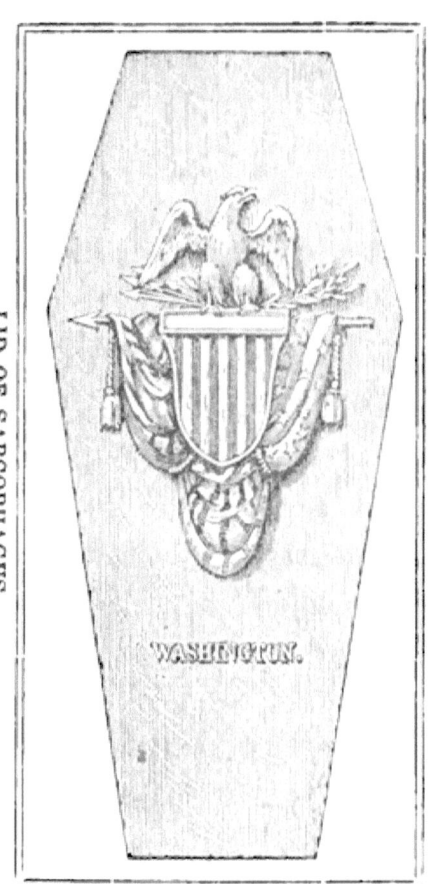

WASHINGTON.

plate, in the shape of the old continental shield or es-cutcheon,* was found, upon which were engraved, in Roman characters, the dates of the birth and death of Washington. This escutcheon was about the size of the palm of a hand, with an ornamental chased border or margin. It had evidently been attached to the leaden lid, but from some cause or other it had given way, and was found between the fragments of the ex-terior wooden case or covering."

---

* The common impression of a heart. The words upon it were as follows: "George Washington, born Feb. 22, 1732, died Dec. 14, 1799." This plate also was deposited in the marble sarcophagus.

XII.

Mrs. Martha Washington.

"And with him, at his side,
There rests the loveliest of her clime,
His bosom friend and sainted bride—
Death's dream, oh how sublime!
Responsive still to memory's magic chime!"

On the left of the gateway, by the side of Washington, rest the remains of his beloved wife, Mrs. Martha Custis Washington, in a marble sarcophagus sculptured by the same hand, in a plain style; and upon it are the words, "Martha, consort of Washington: died May 21, 1801, aged 71 years." Her remains were placed, agreeably to her directions previously to her death, in a leaden coffin, and entombed by the side of her husband in the old vault. Since then they have been removed whenever and wherever her partner's have been.

On the 23d of December, 1799, Mr. Marshall offered the following resolution in Congress: "That a marble monument be erected by the United States, in the Capitol, at the city of Washington, and that the family of General Washington be requested to permit his body to be deposited under it, and that the monument be so designed as to commemorate the great events of his military and political life." To a letter from the Pres-

48

ident of the United States communicating this resolution, Mrs. Washington responded as follows:

MT. VERNON, *December* 31, 1799.

SIR: While I feel, with keenest anguish, the late dispensation of Divine Providence, I cannot be insensible to the mournful tributes of respect and veneration which are paid to the memory of my deceased husband; and, as his best services and most anxious wishes were always devoted to the welfare and happiness of his country, to know that they were really appreciated and gratefully remembered affords no inconsiderable consolation.

Taught by that great example which I have so long had before me never to oppose my private wishes to the public will, I must consent to the request of Congress, which you have had the goodness to transmit to me; and, in doing this, I need not, I cannot, say what a sacrifice of individual feeling I make to a sense of public duty.

With grateful acknowledgments and unfeigned thanks for the personal respect and evidences of condolence expressed by Congress and yourself, I remain, very respectfully, sir, your most obedient humble servant,

MARTHA WASHINGTON.

To the PRESIDENT OF THE U. S.

It is doubtful whether his or her remains could find a more appropriate resting-place than amid Mount Vernon's sacred shades, where no sound of angry passion or political strife disturbs their quiet repose.

She partook in life of the same complacent dignity and even temperament as her husband. She betrayed no wish to interrupt his plans, but rather gave him encouragement in all his undertakings for his country's welfare. Whilst he was in the field, she was employing her time and means, in conjunction with other ladies, to provide food and clothing for the soldiers, and even went from door to door to enlist co-operation in the accomplishment of this laudable design.

Her virtues, her accomplishments, and her lively sympathy with the cause to which her illustrious partner was devoted, doubtless tended greatly to encourage his patriotic zeal and nerve his heart for the trying scenes through which he was called to pass.

XIII.

𝔐onuments.

On the right of the walk leading to the tomb from
the landing is a monument erected to the memory of
Judge Bushrod Washington and his wife, Anna Blackburn. These words are upon its side facing the tomb,
"Within the vault lie buried the mortal remains of
Bushrod Washington, an Associate Justice of the Supreme Court of the United States. He died in Philadelphia, November 26th, 1829, aged 68. By his side
is interred his devoted wife, Anna Blackburn, who sur-
vived her husband but two days, aged 60.

'The heart was broken and aches no more.'
'They were lovely and pleasant in their lives, and in death
they were not divided.' "

Immediately opposite, on the left side of the walk, is
a monument erected to the memory of John A. Washington, (the 2d.) These words are upon its side facing
the tomb : " Sacred to the memory of John A. Washington, son of Corbin and Hannah Washington, and
nephew of Judge Bushrod Washington, who appointed him one of his executors, and bequeathed
him Mount Vernon, where he died, June 16th, 1832,
aged 43."

On the side facing the monument of Bushrod and
Anna Blackburn Washington, are the following words :
"His mortal remains are interred within the vault, and
this humble monument to his worth, his purity, and
unostentatious excellence in all the relations of life, is
erected by his widow."

At the right of the tomb are two monuments enclosed
with iron railings.   One was erected to the memory of
Eleanor Parke Lewis, grand-daughter of General Washington, and has these words inscribed upon it : "Reared
under the roof of the Father of his Country, this lady
was not more marked, while living, for her beauty of person than for the superiority of her mind.   She lived to
be admired, and died to be regretted, in the 74th year
of her age."   The other is, "Sacred to the memory of
Mrs. M. E. A. Conrad, wife of Charles, of New Orleans,
and daughter of Charles and Eleanor P. Lewis, and
grand-niece of General Washington, born April 1st,
1813, at Wooddown, Fairfax county, Va., and died
September 21st, 1839, at Pass Christian, Miss., in the
27th year of her age."

XIV.

The Tomb.

"The echoes of its vaults are eloquent!
    The stones have voices, and the walls do live;
    It is the house of Memory."

The tomb of Washington must ever be regarded as a sacred spot. A halo of glory encircles it. It has a thousand tongues, speaking silently to the heart, and proclaiming, in sweet accents, all the associations of his great name, which is baptized with the everlasting gratitude of his people.

Nothing could exceed the deep feelings of veneration and reverence experienced as we approached the hallowed soil where rest the ashes of him who was "first in war, first in peace, and first in the hearts of his countrymen." At the time, the heavens were most propitious; the sun shone forth with a peculiar beauty and loveliness; the sky was blue, deep, and lofty, its heavenly arch spanning a rich and variegated land-scape. As we stood in front of the tomb, with the Potomac glimmering in the sunlight below, there was around a calm in nature, betokening solemnity in pre-sence of the illustrious dead. Silence reigned, save only as now and then the murmur of the breeze playing over the hills, and the rustling of the winds in the low tree tops, were heard, in gentle minstrelsy to him who reposes amid these august shades.

Washington came upon the stage of action when the world most needed such a man. The golden era was about to dawn in which man was to step beyond the limits within which he had been so long confined. The rights of the many required to be vindicated against the tyranny of the few, and he was to be the chosen leader in the mighty conflict.

He saw, in his prophetic vision, as the clouds of ages rolled away, a beautiful female form, with hope beaming from her lovely brow. For her defence she wore a shield; the stripes emblazoned thereon were emblematic of oppression—the stars, of her ultimate dominion. Heroes fought for her, and maidens wove chaplets and spread garlands in her pathway. Washington beheld the glorious vision, and called it LIBERTY—the spirit of his beloved country. Finding, as he consulted the records of aristocracy and despotism, that they comprised a history of injustice, rapacity, and blood, he vowed "hostility to every form of tyranny over the mind of man;" and, adopting the motto that "all men are created free and equal," being endowed by their Creator with the inalienable rights of "life, liberty, and the pursuit of happiness," he became the chief among that band of heroes who nobly pledged their "lives, their fortunes, and their sacred honors" to the maintenance of the position they had assumed.

Washington well deserves the appellation of the Father of his Country. He commanded with surpassing adeptness, his country's armies; he trained them in the mystery of warfare; confirmed their dubious resolution by his invincible courage; and taught them to be magnanimous in the cheering hour of victory. While his brilliant successes in the army, and his great constitutional and political teachings, standing out in bold relief, command the admiration of the world and are emblazoned upon the pages of history, his quiet disposition, his modest pretensions, and his undaunted perseverance in the most retired walks of life, no less endear him to the hearts of all.

XV.

Personal Appearance.

In the prime of life Washington measured (without shoes) six feet one inch; four years previous to his death, (1795,) six feet one-half inch. He was erect and well proportioned in his person, slightly corpulent. His complexion was florid. His forehead not extremely broad, but well formed. His nose prominent and somewhat aquiline. A firm expression of mouth, indicative of silent habit. His countenance, bearing the impress of intelligence and meditation, indicated a pleasant disposition within. His eyes were dark blue, and his hair of a brown color. His lips expressed good will and kindness. His manners never failed to engage respect and esteem from all who had intercourse with him. He was quite accessible and pleasant in conversation, but cautious in expressing an opinion which he thought it prudent to conceal. The signet of brilliant genius was not so fully stamped upon his mind as correct judgment and consummate prudence. He was not so pre-eminent for possessing any single quality in the highest degree as for that combination of all the elements of greatness which is so seldom found in the same individual.

"He was not only distinguished for his bravery and intelligence, but for the purest virtues which can adorn the human heart. He has been venerated in the memory of distant nations, and immortalized by the blessings he shed upon his country. He resembles the orb of day, imparting his twilight long after he is set, and invisibly dispensing his light and cheering warmth to the world. Cautious and prudent, he was never surprised by the most disheartening failures, nor alarmed into compliance by the most undaunted threats."

XVI.

A Tribute.

The following tribute from Phillips, an Irishman, does justice to the heart and head of the writer:

"It matters very little what immediate spot may have been the birth-place of such a man as Washington. No people can claim, no country can appropriate him. The boon of Providence to the human race, his fame is eternity, and his residence creation. Though it was the defeat of our arms, and the disgrace of our policy, I almost bless the convulsion in which he had his origin. If the heavens thundered, and the earth rocked, yet, when the storm had passed, how pure was the climate that it cleared! how bright, in the brow of the firmament, was the planet which it revealed to us! In the production of Washington, it does really appear as if Nature was endeavoring to improve upon herself, and that all the virtues of the ancient world were but so many studies preparatory to the patriot of the new. Individual instances, no doubt, there were, splendid exemplifications of some singular qualification: Cæsar was merciful, Scipio was continent, Hannibal was patient; but it was reserved for Washington to blend them all in one, and, like the lovely masterpiece of the

Grecian artist, to exhibit, in one glow of associated beauty, the pride of every model, and the perfection of every master. As a general, he marshalled the peasant into a veteran, and supplied by discipline the absence of experience ; as a statesman, he enlarged the policy of the cabinet into the most comprehensive system of general advantage ; and such were the wisdom of his views and the philosophy of his councils, that to the soldier and the statesman he almost added the character of the sage ! A conqueror, he was untainted with the crime of blood. A revolutionist, he was free from every stain of treason ; for aggression commenced the contest, and his country called him to the command. Liberty unsheathed his sword, necessity stained, victory returned it. If he had paused here, history might have doubted what station to assign him ; whether at the head of her citizens or her soldiers, her heroes or her patriots. But the last glorious act crowns his career, and banishes all hesitation. Who, like Washington, after having emancipated a hemisphere, resigned its crowns, and preferred the retirement of domestic life to the adoration of a land he might be almost said to have created? Happy, proud America ! The lightning of heaven yielded to your philosophy ! The temptations of earth could not seduce your patriotism !''

XVII.

Washington's Last Days.

"Oh! shade of the Mighty, how calm is that sleep
   In which Death with his pitiless fetters has bound thee,
While a nation of Freemen their love-watches keep,
   With HENRY and JEFFERSON waiting around thee!"

It was customary, when at home, for Washington to
ride out on horseback around his estate during part of
each day. This he did on the 12th of December,
(Thursday,) and spent several hours riding about to
inspect his farms and give directions to his overseers;
and while returning home late in the afternoon, he was
exposed to falling weather—hail, snow, and rain—which
caused his hair and neck to get wet, and his person
chilled. The next day, the 13th, (Friday,) it was also
his purpose to ride out, but a heavy snow-fall that
morning prevented him. He complained lightly of a
sore throat from his exposure the day previous, yet he
did not seem apprehensive of any danger from it. He
went in the afternoon in front of the house some
distance towards the river, to mark some trees that
were to be cut down in order to make an ornamental
improvement; then returned and passed the evening
with the family in the usual manner. The next morning, which was Saturday, the 14th, between two and

three o'clock, he called his wife and told her his condition. She noticed that he breathed with great difficulty and had considerable hoarseness in speaking. According to his request, she sent for one of the overseers to bleed him. The family became alarmed when they saw the rapid advancement of the disease. A messenger was despatched for the family physician, Dr. Craik, who resided in Alexandria. In the meantime, another messenger went for Dr. Brown, who lived nearer Mount Vernon. They arrived during the morning, and in the course of the day Dr. Dick was also called in; but the skill of the physicians, though exerted to the utmost, proved insufficient to arrest his disease—quinsy.

As dissolution was fast approaching, he endeavored to raise himself up in bed, when Dr. Craik held out his hand and assisted him. He then cast a benign look around the room, and said to the physicians, "I feel myself going: I thank you for your attention; but I pray you take no more trouble about me. Let me go off quietly; I cannot last long."

XVIII.

Washington's Death.

About ten o'clock in the evening he made several fruitless efforts to converse with some of those around the bedside. At length he succeeded in saying, "I am just going; have me decently buried, and do not let my body be put into the vault in less than three days after I am dead."

Mr. Tobias Lear, who was for many years Washington's secretary, and afterwards superintendent of his private affairs, being present during Washington's last illness, says: "About ten minutes before he expired, which was between ten and eleven o'clock, his breathing became easier. He lay quietly; he withdrew his hand from mine and felt his own pulse. I saw his countenance change. I spoke to Dr. Craik, who sat by the fire. He came to the bedside. The General's hand fell from his wrist. I took it in mine, and pressed it to my bosom. Dr. Craik put his hands over his eyes, and he expired without a struggle or a sigh. While we were fixed in silent grief, Mrs. Washington, who was sitting at the foot of the bed, asked, with a firm and collected voice, 'Is he gone?' I could not speak, but held up my hand as a signal that he was no more. ''Tis

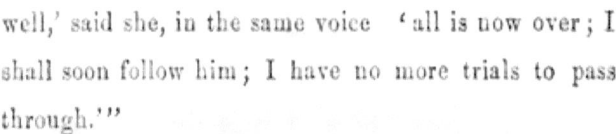
well,' said she, in the same voice 'all is now over; I shall soon follow him; I have no more trials to pass through.'"

Thus did the great man fall asleep, to wake no more on earth; but his spirit winged its flight to happier realms. He died on Saturday night, December 14th, 1799.

The painful news of the death of Washington arrived at the seat of government (Philadelphia) before the information of his sickness. It caused a general gloom to pervade the minds of the members of Congress. Silence reigned in the House of Representatives for a short period, after which Mr. Marshall, (who afterwards became Chief Justice of the Supreme Court of the United States,) with a voice and countenance indicative of the deepest sorrow, commenced an address to the House, as follows: "Mr. Speaker, information has just been received that our illustrious citizen, the Commander-in-Chief of the American army and the late President of the United States, is no more. Though this distressing intelligence is not certain, there is too much reason to believe its truth. After receiving information of this national calamity, so heavy and afflicting, the House of Representatives can be but ill fitted for public business. I move you, therefore, that we adjourn." The House adjourned immediately, as also did the Senate.

The next morning, in the House, Mr. Marshall addressed the chair in the following manner:

"Mr. SPEAKER: The melancholy event, which was yesterday announced with doubt, has been rendered too certain. Our Washington is no more! The hero, the patriot, and the sage of America; the man on whom in times of danger every eye was turned and all hopes were placed, lives now only in his own great actions and in the hearts of an affectionate and afflicted people.

"If, sir, it had even not been usual openly to testify respect for the memory of those whom Heaven has selected as its instruments for dispensing good to man, yet such has been the uncommon worth and such the extraordinary incidents which have marked the life of him whose loss we all deplore, that the whole American nation, impelled by the same feelings, would call with one voice for a public manifestation of that sorrow which is so deep and so universal.

"More than any other individual, and as much as to one individual was possible, has he contributed to found this our wide-spreading empire, and to give to the western world independence and freedom. Having effected the great object for which he was placed at the head of our armies, we have seen him convert the sword into the ploughshare, and sink the soldier in the citizen.

"When the debility of our federal system had become manifest, and the bonds which connected this vast continent were dissolving, we have seen him the chief of those patriots who formed for us a constitution, which, by preserving the union, will, I trust, substantiate and perpetuate those blessings which our Revolution had promised to bestow.

"In obedience to the general voice of this country, calling him to preside over a great people, we have seen him once more quit the retirement he loved, and, in a season more stormy and tempestuous than war itself, with calm and wise determination pursue the true interests of the nation, and contribute, more than any other could contribute, to the establishment of that system of policy which will, I trust, yet preserve our peace, our honor, and our independence.

"Having been twice unanimously chosen the Chief Magistrate of a free people, we have seen him, at a time when his re-election with universal suffrage could not be doubted, afford to the world a rare instance of moderation, by withdrawing from his station to the peaceful walks of private life.

"However the public confidence may change and the

public affections fluctuate with respect to others, with respect to him they have, in war and in peace, in public and private life, been as steady as his own firm mind and as constant as his own exalted virtues."

He then offered three resolutions, which passed. Among the rest it was resolved, in conjunction with the Senate, that there be appointed a committee to consider the most appropriate manner of paying honor to the memory of the man first in war, first in peace, and first in the hearts of his countrymen. The resolutions had no sooner passed, than a message was received from the President of the United States, John Adams, transmitting a letter from Mr. T. Lear, " which," said the message, "will inform you that it had pleased Divine Providence to remove from this life our excellent fellow-citizen, George Washington, by the purity of his life and a long series of services to his country rendered illustrious through the world. It remains for an affectionate and grateful people, in whose hearts he can never die, to pay suitable honor to his memory."

On this mournful event the Senate addressed a long letter to the President. It closed as follows: "This event, so distressing to all our fellow-citizens, must be peculiarly heavy to you, who have long been associated with him in deeds of patriotism. Permit us, sir, to

mingle our tears with yours. On this occasion it is manly to weep. To lose such a man, at such a crisis, is no common calamity to the world Our country mourns a father. The Almighty dispenser of human events has taken from us our greatest benefactor and ornament. It becomes us to submit with reverence to Him who 'maketh darkness his pavilion.'"

XIX.

The Burial.

The arrangements of the funeral procession were made by Colonels Little, Sims, and Deneale, and Dr. Dick; and 12 o'clock on Wednesday, December 18th, was the appointed hour to bury the body; but as some of the military troops from a distance failed to arrive at the hour, and persons were coming in from various quarters, the hour was postponed. Between 2 and 3 o'clock p. m. a signal gun was heard from a vessel moored near the river shore, in solemn token that the funeral cortege was in readiness to start.

The procession moved out through the gate in the rear of the house, left wing, and proceeded around to the east or river front, along the right wing, down the lawn, to the old family vault, in the following order:

Cavalry, infantry, and guard, with arms reversed;
Music;
Clergy, consisting of Rev. Messrs. Davies, Muir,
Moffat, and Addison;
The General's horse, with his saddle, holsters and pistols,
the horse being led by two grooms, dressed
in black, named Cyrus and Wilson;
Colonel Blackburn, preceding the corpse;

Pall Bearers.		Pall Bearers.
Col. SIMS,		Col. GILPIN,
Col. RAMSAY, ⟩ CORPSE. ⟨		Col. MARSTELLER,
Col. PAYNE,		Col. LITTLE.

Principal Mourners.
Misses Nancy and Sally Stuart;
Miss Fairfax and Miss Denison;
Messrs. Law and Peter;
Dr. Craik and Mr. Lear;
Lord Fairfax and Ferdinando Fairfax;
Lodge No. 23 of the Free Masons;
Corporation of Alexandria;
Citizens, preceded by Mr Anderson and the overseers.

As soon as the head of the procession had arrived at the bottom of the lawn, near the family vault, the cavalry halted and then formed their lines; the infantry did the same; immediately after, the clergy, masonic brothers, and citizens descended to the vault, when the Rev. Mr. Davis read the funeral services of the church, and pronounced a short address; after which the masonic brethern performed their ceremonies, and deposited the corpse in the vault. A general discharge of guns from the military that lined the banks of the river closed the scene.

The coffin bore the following inscriptions: at the head, " Surge ad Judicum ;" about the middle, " Gloria Deo ;" and on the ornamental silver plate, " General George Washington departed this life on the 14th December 1799. Æt. 68."

He expressed in his will the desire that he should be buried in a private manner, and without any parade or funeral oration ; but in this instance his fellow-citizens could not be dissuaded from going contrary to his wish, and therefore assembled in great numbers to pay their last tribute of respect to his earthly remains.

The proud fleet of the English, coming up the Potomac river, in hostile aspect, in the time of the last war, halted in front of Mount Vernon, and, amid the curling smoke of their minute guns, testified their respect for the memory of our illustrious Washington—

"Great, without pomp; without ambition, brave;
Proud, not to conquer fellow-men, but save."

www.ingramcontent.com/pod-product-compliance
Lightning Source LLC
Chambersburg PA
CBHW022009050726
47499CB00008BA/2732